Rosetown Summer

Also by Cynthia Rylant

Missing May

When I Was Young in the Mountains

Gooseberry Park

Gooseberry Park and the Master Plan

The Henry & Mudge series

Life

The Mr. Putter & Tabby series

The Old Woman Who Named Things

The Van Gogh Cafe

The Lighthouse Family series

God Got a Dog

Rosetown

The Motor Mouse Books

Cynthia Rylant

BEACH LANE BOOKS

New York London Toronto Sydney New Delhi

BEACH LANE BOOKS

An imprint of Simon & Schuster Children's Publishing Division

1230 Avenue of the Americas, New York, New York 10020

Text © 2021 by Cynthia Rylant

Jacket illustration © 2021 by Lori Richmond

Jacket design by Sonia Chaghatzbanian © 2021 by Simon & Schuster, Inc.

For information about special discounts for bulk purchases, please contact Simon & Schuster Special Sales at 1-866-506-1949 or business@simonandschuster.com.

The Simon & Schuster Speakers Bureau can bring authors to your live event. For more information or to book an event, contact the Simon & Schuster Speakers Bureau at 1-866-248-3049 or visit our website at www.simonspeakers.com.

Interior design by Irene Metaxatos

The text for this book was set in ITC Century Std.

Manufactured in the United States of America / 0621 FFG / First Edition

10 9 8 7 6 5 4 3 2 1

Library of Congress Cataloging-in-Publication Data

Names: Rylant, Cynthia, author.

Title: Rosetown summer / Cynthia Rylant.

Description: First edition. | New York : Beach Lane Books, [2021] | Sequel to: Rosetown. | Audience: Ages 8-12. | Audience: Grades 4-6. | Summary: In 1973, Flora loves living in the quiet town of Rosetown, Indiana, where change is not constant, but life takes a decided turn during the summer between fourth and fifth grades.

Identifiers: LCCN 2020052194 (print) | LCCN 2020052195 (ebook) | ISBN 9781534494718 (hardcover) | ISBN 9781534494732 (ebook)

Subjects: CYAC: Friendship—Fiction. | Change—Fiction. | City and town life—Indiana—Fiction. | Indiana—History—20th century—Fiction.

Classification: LCC PZ7.R982 Rs 2021 (print) | LCC PZ7.R982 (ebook) | DDC [Fic]—dc23

LC record available at https://lccn.loc.gov/2020052194

LC ebook record available at https://lccn.loc.gov/2020052195

To Judy Rule
in Huntington, West Virginia . . .
for all the years
helping a library grow

1

Rosetown Paper and Press sat on Main Street in Rosetown, Indiana, and it was one of Flora Smallwood's favorite places to be. The shop belonged to Flora's mother and father, and all of its beautiful cards and calendars and journals had been printed on an old-fashioned letterpress in the back room. It was comforting to be among all of the lovely messages: *A garden of wishes for you. You are my cup of tea. To my very dearest dear.* And to trace a finger over the little birds, the garlands of ivy, the blue forget-me-nots and other pretty decorations on the papers.

The shop was new—it had been open only for a month—but as one might say of a special friend, it seemed to Flora that she had known it forever.

August in Indiana always had a stillness that Flora appreciated, as she was herself a mostly still person. She was sure this was why her cat, Serenity, loved her so much. Cats enjoy quiet people. And Serenity had been a stray cat when Flora and her friend Yury had found her. Serenity had been through enough challenges in her kitty life and now wanted nothing more than to be with a gentle person who did not fidget. Flora fit this description perfectly.

When the school year had ended in June, Flora and her friends Nessy and Yury had all launched immediately into their summer projects, and those projects were continuing with great success.

Yury and his dog, Friday, were now in the Beginner class at the Good Manners for Good Dogs dog school, having passed puppy class to great applause (Flora's). After dog school on Saturday mornings, Yury and Flora still sat on the bench outside the

Peaceable Buns Bakery, sharing muffins and talking, as Friday chewed on leftover crusts provided by the friendly bakers. Beginner class was more rigorous than puppy school, and Yury always had much to say about the morning's class. ("Friday sat fine, but Skippy behind us kept rolling over.")

Nessy, who at nine was a year younger than Flora, was continuing the piano lessons she and Flora had started many months before. Nessy was a natural musician (unlike Flora, who was happy to play old folk songs forever while Nessy dove into Mozart), and with the windows of her home wide open for the summer, Nessy's playing was enjoyed by her neighbors, all of whom agreed she had "a remarkable talent." Nessy didn't care about talent, though. She just wanted to play piano while her little canary, Sunny, sang along. And when Nessy wasn't practicing the piano, she was practicing riding a pink bicycle with white streamers and a bell and a basket, in which she always carried her doll Happy Girl. Nessy was cautious about this new bicycle—it had taken much encouragement from Flora for Nessy to even think about riding a bicycle—but with the help of Happy Girl, Nessy was doing fine.

And Flora was still assisting her parents at the paper shop, though not nearly as energetically as in June and July. In June they had received the keys to the empty storefront on Main Street, and for the first week they cleaned, the second week they painted, the third week they carried in furniture and equipment (Flora's job that week had been to bring lunch), and the final week her parents finally printed their first products to sell to the public. The letterpress was louder than Flora had expected, so she stayed at home with Serenity and read during the hours of printing. But in the late afternoon, after the noise had stopped, she took Serenity to the upper floor of the shop so they could sit on the wicker daybed by the window and watch the pigeons.

July had been something of a whirlwind, with the shop open part-time and her parents adjusting their schedules. (Flora's father was still a full-time photographer for the *Rosetown Chronicle*.) Flora was especially busy with errands that month, and she'd made quite a few trips to the Peaceable Buns Bakery on everyone's behalf.

These had been hectic months, so they passed quickly, but—besides the new paper shop—there hadn't been much real change in Rosetown.

But now, with only a month to go before school would start, there was talk of another change, the subject of which Flora found deeply concerning. It involved her dearest place, the special destination she had shared with her friend Yury so many school-day afternoons: Wings and a Chair Used Books. It was at this shop that Flora and Yury's friendship had planted its roots and where a purple velveteen chair in the front window always beckoned them in.

The bookshop's owner, Miss Meriwether, had been invited by a friend to come live together on a farm in Montana in the Bitterroot Valley. And she was considering it. This was all that Flora knew.

And she wondered: If Wings and a Chair changed, what else might?

2

Flora had received her first journal in June as soon as the pages came off the letterpress and were stitched together and finished with a beautiful cover: an owl. Her father had handed her the journal and said, "You finished fourth grade and you rescued a nice cat. This is to celebrate both."

Flora had shyly accepted the very first journal made at Rosetown Paper and Press.

"Yury says I should write stories," Flora said. "But I'd rather read them."

Her father nodded. "I'd rather look at photographs than take them," he said.

"Really?" asked Flora.

"But I guess if all photographers felt that way," answered her father, "we wouldn't have any photographs to look at."

Flora was silent a moment. She would have to think about that idea later when she had time to separate the words. Some ideas were so complicated that she had to pick the words apart later like a handful of flowers.

"I love the owl," she said.

In that moment Flora could not have imagined that, when she was finally ready to write in her journal, the first thing she would tell it was that Miss Meriwether might be leaving.

Flora was sensitive about anyone or anything leaving. She was sensitive about change. That was why she wanted to stay forever in Rosetown, which had hardly changed in a hundred years. It was an old town, a historic town, just the town she needed.

And change had been painful for her, not so long

ago. She would never forget their dear old dog, Laurence, passing away last summer. Sometimes she thought of him and felt almost as sad as she had when he left.

Then soon after Laurence was gone, her parents—Forster and Emma Jean—had decided to live in separate houses. Flora spent all of fourth grade walking back and forth between them, carrying Serenity in her kitty travel box. That change had also been a terrible change, at first. But just as she had become adjusted to living in both a white house and a yellow house, and had felt it would be all right, her parents decided not only to live together in just one house again—the white one—but to open a shop together, Rosetown Paper and Press.

Everything had worked out even better than Flora had imagined it could, but inside her was still that tender memory of the first day her family lived in separate houses, that tender, sensitive memory of pain.

Flora's mother still worked three afternoons

8

each week at Wings and a Chair, and both Flora and her mother loved Miss Meriwether and her exuberant free spirit. Miss Meriwether had come back to Rosetown after living an unusual life in many exotic places. She had decided to become a more settled person and open a shop.

From their first meeting on the first day of fourth grade, Flora's and Yury's favorite place to be together had been the Young People's Nook in Miss Meriwether's shop. They had spent many afternoons reading vintage books, and now they often, quite out of the blue, would launch into conversation about an especially exciting turn in the plot of something they had read months earlier: "Remember when Bert Walton was thrown off his horse and chased by a grizzly?"

And for Yury, who had emigrated from the Ukraine, every adventure book, mystery—even the books about chickens and crickets—helped him build a history, his own history, in America.

The bookshop had, in many ways, become their

story, Flora and Yury's. Every story needs a setting and a beginning, and Wings and a Chair had given them both.

The shop had been a kind of resting place for them as they had made their way through fourth grade. Flora did not have to adjust herself to being there, as she had in her father's separate house and his separate kitchen. As she had in her separate bedroom filled with clothes and books carried over from the other house. And Yury did not have to adjust to being the new boy in a classroom, a new boy from the Ukraine who was learning the rules of the playground and learning who among the students was smartest or strongest or least trust-worthy.

Wings and a Chair had been respite and relief, at first, for them both. How simple and easy to walk there together, find a book, and start a story.

Now, after nearly a year had passed, both Flora and Yury had found their footing: their families were more settled, fourth grade had been con-quered. And the bookshop was now less sanctuary and more habit, like a familiar road one travels each day or a television show one never misses. It was a steady companion, as they were now to each other.

Flora wanted Miss Meriwether to stay.

3

Flora met her best friend Nessy at the Rosetown Free Library when they were five and four, respectively. They were members—at their mothers' urging and confidence—of the Summer Reading Club that summer. The theme of the club that year was Fly to Adventure, and their group—the youngest—was called the Honeybees. During craft time they made paper sets of wings to wear and paper garlands of flowers for the library windows, and they enjoyed little cups of lemonade they pretended was nectar. And, of course, they listened to stories and left for home with at least one borrowed book to read and return.

Even now, when Flora saw a honeybee, she often thought of the library.

Flora had enjoyed being part of the library's Summer Reading Club every summer since then. She had been a Caterpillar, a Porpoise, a Prairie Dog, and an Alpaca. As had Nessy.

This summer, though, the girls had not joined the reading club. Nessy's piano lessons and summer travels with her parents to visit family near and far had kept her quite busy and more than a little disorganized. And Flora's part in helping with the opening of Rosetown Paper and Press had distracted her thoroughly. Flora was easily overloaded by too much activity. Her mother had recently explained to her, in fact, what an "introvert" was and asked her if she thought she might be one.

"Yes," Flora had answered. "And I am pretty sure Serenity is one too."

But Flora did so appreciate the library. The theme this year for summer reading was Great Migrations, and had she joined the club, she would have been a Blue Whale. She had encouraged Yury to join, but Yury wasn't interested, primarily because his Saturdays were taken up with dog school and family time. Yury's father was a doctor and always busy at his office on Main Street all week. So on Saturdays, Yury's family enjoyed seeing a movie together or bowling at Rosetown Lanes. One of the good things about Rosetown was that it was really quite a pleasant place to be on a Saturday.

"I've hardly been to the library this summer," Flora said to her mother one day as they walked past it toward the Windy Day Diner for lunch. Flora's mother was on her way to the paper shop to design cards for the fall season ahead. Flora had suggested some crow cards, and her mother thought that was a good idea. Fall seemed to be a crow's favorite time of year.

"Your father and I have kept you so busy," said Flora's mother. "Mr. Anderson probably misses you in Summer Reading. You always earned so many stickers."

Mr. Anderson was the children's librarian. Like Miss Meriwether at the bookshop, Mr. Anderson loved being around people and books. He was a big person with a big smile, and even the shyest children warmed to him right away. He kept a hedgehog in the Children's Room, and every year there was a contest to name it. The hedgehog would have the name for a year. Then a new person would win the contest, and the hedgehog would become somebody else. Its current name was Miss Sissy. Its previous name had been Frank Smith. The name contest was quite popular.

"I like the library so much that I would work there for free," said Flora.

"Well, maybe you could do that now," said Emma Jean as they entered the diner.

"What do you mean?" asked Flora. "I'm only ten."

They slid into an empty booth and pulled out menus from behind the condiments rack.

Flora's mother smiled. "I know how old you are," she said. "Let's decide what we'd like."

Flora knew what she wanted, as she always

15

ordered the same thing: a grilled cheese sandwich and a root beer float.

Her mother never knew what she wanted, so Flora had to wait. When finally the young waitress had taken their orders—after commenting "Love your paper shop!"—they picked up their conversation again.

"Well, the shop is up and running, so your father and I don't need as much help," said Flora's mother. "You have more free time. Maybe you could volunteer in the Children's Room? I'm sure Mr. Anderson is very busy now."

"But I'm ten," said Flora.

"Yes, you are," said her mother, smiling again. "And what I know about small children is that they love bigger children. And are usually very good when a big child is watching over and helping them."

Flora thought on this for a few moments.

"I followed cousin Kate around everywhere when we visited Aunt Jane," she said.

"Yes," answered her mother. "You were three and Kate was nine."

"Nine?" repeated Flora. "She seemed so much older."

"I guess nine seems old when someone is three," said Emma Jean, reaching for a tea bag and the mug of hot water just set down in front of her.

"You mean I could maybe help with the little children?" asked Flora. "At the library?"

"Perhaps you could ask Mr. Anderson if he needs an assistant at Toddler Story Time," said Flora's mother. "Maybe you could help with the crafts. Toddlers are pretty unpredictable when paper and glue are involved."

The waitress set a grilled cheese sandwich and a float in front of Flora.

"Thank you," Flora said.

She looked at her mother. "Have you been thinking about this for a while?" Flora asked.

"I sometimes have inspirations," said her mother.

Flora nodded. "It's because you have a good imagination," she told her mother. "There's a line in *The Mystery Horse* about imagination: *Imagination is a wonderful thing, Elizabeth. But you will have to control it.*"

"That's probably just the sort of thing someone with no imagination would say," Flora added.

The subject of books and imagination brought Flora back to the worry that seemed always on her mind in recent days.

"Is Miss Meriwether going to move away?" she asked her mother. Flora wasn't sure she really wanted to know the answer. When a question is so big inside one's mind, sometimes a person does not really want to know its answer.

Her mother sighed. She looked away a moment, then looked back at Flora.

"She seems torn," Flora's mother said. "Miss Meriwether is at one of life's crossroads: to stay or to go. This is a problem many people face."

Flora shook her head. "Not me," she said. "I would always choose to stay."

Her mother smiled. "But if you aren't at a crossroads yet, dear," she said, "how can you know? Sometimes a person really must choose between two good things."

Two good things, thought Flora.

"I would choose the thing that involved a cat," she said.

Her mother laughed.

They both were quiet a moment.

"If the bookshop closed, I would miss the books in the window," Flora said. "And the purple chair. And most of all, Yury."

Her mother looked with concern at Flora's serious face.

"Yury will be your friend whether Miss Meriwether stays or goes," she said to Flora.

Flora was quiet. Her mother did not press her to respond.

Flora looked out the window of the diner and watched the people walking by on their way somewhere. She thought of the months spent walking between the white house and the yellow house. And how it is to be suspended between two things, waiting for someone to make a choice, waiting to know what there is to hold on to and what there is to let go.

4

"Be prepared" were the first words Yury said when he met Flora at the corner of State and Main to walk to Miss Meriwether's bookshop the next day.

"Okay," said Flora.

Flora and Yury shared an interest in survival tactics—Yury's interest was much stronger than hers, as he wanted to live the survival tactics, whereas she mainly just wanted to talk about them—so being prepared was not an uncommon topic between them.

"No, it's the Scout motto," explained Yury as they headed down Main. "Be prepared."

"Boy Scouts?" asked Flora.

Yury nodded.

"And . . . ," Flora said encouragingly.

"I don't know why I never thought of it before," said Yury. "Becoming a Scout."

"Don't they just go camping?" asked Flora. "Didn't you say camping is boring?"

"It's boring with my father and his friend Donald," said Yury. "A doctor and dentist camping, all they want to talk about are the tools. I want to search for edible plants, but they just want to sit in camp chairs and compare Swiss Army knives."

"I'd have gone with you to look for edible plants," said Flora.

"I know," said Yury.

"Do you remember that book from the shop," Yury continued, "*Tom Slade, Boy Scout*?"

"I think I was reading all the Meg books then," said Flora.

"Well, Tom Slade is no Walton boy, I can tell you

that," Yury said. "But there was one line in it that stayed with me."

That sounded familiar. Lines stayed with Flora all the time.

"*A Scout's duty is to help other people at all times*," quoted Yury.

"What does that have to do with camping?" asked Flora. They were nearing the bookshop.

"Nothing. That's my point," answered Yury. "It's the helping part of the Scouts. Helping others is what Search and Rescue is all about."

Search and Rescue was Yury's dream, for him and for his dog, Friday, just as soon as he was old enough. Death Valley. The Everglades. Mount McKinley. Yury's goal was to rescue people in all the dangerous places.

"The Scouts earn merit badges," said Yury. "There are badges for—listen carefully—Transportation of an Injured Person, First Aid for Fractures, Lifesaving. And—you won't believe this—Edible Plants."

They stopped in front of the display window of Wings and a Chair to see if Miss Meriwether had placed anything new there that would be of interest to them.

"It sounds hard," said Flora. "Look, there's a new Dave Porter adventure."

"*Dave Porter at Bear Camp*," read Yury aloud.

"Edible Plants would be fun," Flora continued, getting back to their subject. "But the other badges sound too grown-up."

"The handbook says you proceed at your own speed," said Yury, pushing open the door. "It would probably take me years."

"Hello, you dears!" called Miss Meriwether from the back room. "I hear your voices!"

"And we hear yours!" answered Flora, smiling.

"Did you see the Dave Porter book in the window?" asked Miss Meriwether, coming out to her desk. Flora admired her long flowery skirt and patent leather granny boots. Her dark hair was pulled back into a ponytail as usual. Miss Meriwether always looked unique.

"We did," said Yury. "We're just headed for it now."

"But wait," said Miss Meriwether. "Before the Nook swallows you up, how are you both? Flora?" She looked at Flora with warm interest and joy.

"I might help with Toddler Story Time at the library," said Flora.

"How fabulous!" said Miss Meriwether. "You have just the right vibration for small creatures. They will feel safe with you."

Miss Meriwether was the only person Flora knew who often referred to vibrations.

"Thank you," said Flora.

"And you, Yury?" asked Miss Meriwether. "What mountains are you intending to climb?"

Yury grinned. Miss Meriwether knew he loved a challenge. "Well," Yury said, "I am caught between a knife and a spear."

Flora's eyes grew wide. "*The Pirates of Shan*," she said.

"It's a great line, isn't it?" said Yury.

She nodded.

"I am thinking of joining the Boy Scouts so I can

learn skills for Search and Rescue," Yury explained to Miss Meriwether. "But between here and First Aid for Fractures is an awful lot of camping."

"I'm pretty sure," said Flora, nodding emphatically.

"Camping doesn't call to you?" asked Miss Meriwether.

"Only if it involves plucking someone off a cliff two hundred feet above a raging river," answered Yury.

"Ah, yes," said Miss Meriwether.

"My Zen master," she continued, "would say 'Wait, and more will be revealed' when one is, as you say, caught between a knife and a spear."

Flora suddenly realized that Miss Meriwether herself must be waiting for more to be revealed.

"Now," Miss Meriwether continued, "you two find that Dave Porter book, and before you leave, come and get some cookies in the back room. I made Almond Crescents! They are delicious!"

Flora and Yury got comfortable in the Young

People's Nook, she on a chair, he on the floor.

"Who reads the first chapter?" asked Yury.

"You," said Flora.

Yury cleared his throat to begin.

"I have a feeling she's leaving," Flora said softly.

Yury gave a long sigh. "Me too," he said.

5

The Rosetown Free Library was, Flora thought, the loveliest building in town. It was made of brick, and a tall and impressive flight of stairs led from the sidewalk to the entrance, where a large, heavy wooden door—flanked by two vintage gaslights and two white columns—welcomed everyone inside.

Whenever Flora stepped through that door, she felt a quickening, that special feeling that comes from seeing or hearing something beautiful and uplifting.

The magnificent main room of the library had a very tall ceiling, and there were large windows on all sides, underneath which sat wide bookcases. To the left was the Adult Reading Room and to the right the Children's Room. At the back of the main room was a long mahogany desk where the librarians worked.

Mr. Anderson was hardly ever at that desk. He was captain of the very important ship called the Children's Room, and he abandoned his ship only reluctantly. Flora had never visited the library when he wasn't there in that room, helping a child find a book on fireflies or trains or anything at all interesting, or carefully setting up a display—Lion Books for Lion Fans—or holding up a picture book in the Story Time Corner and reading to a polite group of young patrons, some clutching a doll or a teddy bear or other important companion for going through life and libraries. Mr. Anderson welcomed them all and always remembered the names of dolls and bears, and especially the names of children who stepped into the large, well-lit space looking for something good to read.

Flora's father once, on a visit to the library with

her, told Flora that a wealthy man had given Rose-town this wonderful library. Mr. Andrew Carnegie had donated over two thousand library buildings to towns in America and other countries.

"It is amazing that he found us in Rosetown," Flora said to her father that day.

"Yes, it is," her father had answered.

And now Flora was crossing the main floor of the Rosetown Free Library and entering the Children's Room to the right to see if she might be useful.

"Flora!" said Mr. Anderson when he saw her, and he flashed that big smile that caused all children to smile back. "How are you and your parents and Serenity, and what in the world have you been doing with yourself this summer? Are you still read-ing every cat book you can find?"

Flora smiled and nodded.

"Excellent!" Mr. Anderson said. He slipped the book about volcanoes that he was holding back onto the shelf. Flora took note of it. Yury would probably need to know about volcanoes for Search and Rescue.

"We opened a paper shop," said Flora.

"You did indeed!" said Mr. Anderson. "I saw it! I think letterpress printing is fantastic. I'm going to do all my Christmas shopping there."

"Thank you," said Flora. "We make nice journals. And calendars."

"Exactly," said Mr. Anderson.

Flora took a deep breath and looked around the big sunlit room.

"Mr. Anderson," she began. Then she stopped. She had forgotten how to ask her question. Her mother had helped her, but now she had forgotten.

"Hmmm," Flora said aloud, to no one in particular.

Mr. Anderson smiled and waited.

Flora took the plunge.

"Could I help you with Toddler Story Time until school starts?" she asked, looking partly at his large friendly face and partly at the craft table in the far corner.

"I am good with glue," she added.

Mr. Anderson hesitated for just a moment, and then he laughed.

"You're hired!" he said. "I am terrible with glue!"

"Really?" asked Flora.

"It seems no one has left town for vacation this summer and instead everyone is vacationing at the library," said Mr. Anderson. "I have toddlers up to my ears on Monday mornings."

"Really?" Flora repeated.

"Yes," said Mr. Anderson. "They sit very well for a story. But it is a challenge for one librarian to help so many little hands glue feathers to a chicken. So to speak."

He laughed.

"It does sound tricky," Flora said with a grin.

"Maybe you can help out next Monday?" Mr. Anderson continued. "I'll have them making lettuces and carrots from Mr. McGregor's garden, and heaven knows I'll need someone good with glue."

"I'd love to," said Flora.

And there and then, in the space between Mr. McGregor's lettuces and "I'd love to," something happened for Flora. Life turned a small moment into a vision, and she knew what she wanted to be when she grew up: a librarian!

But for now, she intended to be a very good Story Time assistant.

6

Flora loved to visit Nessy at Nessy's house in the gated community. Living in a newly built house in a newly built neighborhood behind a newly built gate did not appeal to Flora since she was—as her mother once described her—"a child of the Nineteenth Century." But Flora did love to visit.

And the community suited Nessy and her parents fine. Her father liked the fancy gate, her mother liked the modern houses, and Nessy liked the privacy. If she was going to be the rider of a bicycle, Nessy needed a neighborhood that saw hardly any movement besides that of tiny birds and sometimes a confused deer. Nessy had been so uncertain of her abilities on a bicycle that, had she not lived in a gated community, the white streamers and the bell and the basket for Happy Girl would probably never have found their way into her life.

As it turned out, though, Nessy did learn to ride, she did become certain of her abilities, and the dinging of her bicycle bell was now a sweet and constant sound in her neighborhood on warm summer mornings.

Early on Tuesday, Flora's father dropped Flora at Nessy's house to spend the day. Everyone had been so busy this summer, and Flora and Nessy needed some playtime together. School would start before too long, and since they were in different grades, the girls wouldn't see much of each other during school hours. And because Nessy rode the school bus home after school, they wouldn't even have a chance to walk home together. Flora loved being able to walk home from school. She loved being under the leaves of the old walnut and oak trees along the streets. She loved the front porches and the lily gardens. And the shy dog waiting behind a picket fence to be petted.

Nessy didn't mind taking the school bus. But when Flora watched it roll away, she was always glad she wasn't on it.

Flora's father stepped out of the car to say hello to Nessy's mother while Flora retrieved her doll case from the backseat. She and Nessy still loved to play with dolls, and Flora's doll, Charlotte, had so many different clothes, which had been sewn by Flora's mother, that Nessy often asked Flora to bring her doll with her. Happy Girl enjoyed trying on new dresses and bonnets.

"Hello, Flora! Hello, Forster!" said Nessy's mother when she opened the front door. Naturally she'd been watching for them, as she was the person who had buzzed them through the gate.

Nessy stood beside her mother and grinned at Flora. They were so happy to see each other, and both wanted to run immediately to the den to play. But they waited until Flora's father gave Flora a hug, thanked Nessy's mother for inviting her, and started walking back to his car.

"Let's go!" said Nessy.

The girls ran down the hall and into the den, where two of the loveliest things in Nessy's life could be found: her piano and her canary. Sunny was immediately thrilled to see not just one girl but two, and he hopped from perch to perch in his large cage and rang his little bird bell and flew from one corner to the other, telling them all his news with melodic chirps and trills.

"Oh, Sunny," said Flora, putting her face up to the cage near his, "I've missed you!"

"I found out he likes honeydew melon," said Nessy.

Flora smiled. "Me too," she said.

"We can all have some with lunch," added Nessy.

"Okay," answered Flora. "But I get to sit next to Sunny."

Nessy giggled.

They took their dolls out to the patio to play. Flora did appreciate this feature of a modern house: a covered patio with a big round table just right for laying out doll dresses and bonnets.

"Flora, I waited until you got here to tell you something," Nessy said with a serious tone.

Oh dear, thought Flora. "You're not moving away, are you, Nessy?" she asked softly.

"Oh no!" Nessy said. "My father says we are never moving again. He does not like packing boxes."

"Thank goodness," said Flora, wishing Miss Meriwether were cut from the same cloth.

"It's about camp," said Nessy, looking worried.

"Camp?" repeated Flora. "Nessy, are you sure you want to go to camp? It's sort of messy."

Nessy smiled. "It's not that kind of camp," she said. "This is music camp. At the high school. I don't know why they call it camp, but they do."

"Music camp!" said Flora. "Do you want to go?"

"No, I don't want to go at all!" Nessy said with conviction. She held Happy Girl closer.

"But it's not an overnight camp," Nessy continued. "I get to come home on a bus every day in time for dinner."

"You're right," said Flora. "I don't know why they call it a camp either if you come home on a bus for dinner.

"But that's good!" Flora added. "You won't have to miss Sunny too much!"

Nessy still looked unhappy. "I really do not want to go at all," she said. "I want to stay home."

Flora sighed and patted Nessy's hand. Flora so well understood wanting to be home. Especially with someone who loved you. Like a white cat with a yellow tip on its tail. Or a small yellow bird full of song.

But Flora had a feeling that music camp would be important for Nessy. She had a feeling that Nessy should go.

Then she had an idea.

"Nessy, remember when Miss Meriwether said she would take us someday to the glass conservatory in Indianapolis to see the tropical plants?" asked Flora.

Nessy nodded.

"Well," continued Flora, "if you go to music

camp—which would be brave—maybe Miss Meri-wether would take us to the conservatory to cele-brate when you're finished!"

Nessy's eyes were wide as she stared at Flora. Nessy loved plants. She wanted to be a gardener when she grew up.

"Do you think she would?" asked Nessy, hugging Happy Girl even tighter.

Flora remembered the time Miss Meriwether had suddenly flown to Paris on a whim. She remem-bered the miniature conservatory she had seen once when she and her mother had visited Miss Meriwether in her apartment. And she also remem-bered Miss Meriwether's generous heart.

"Yes!" said Flora. "I think she would!"

"Okay," said Nessy, and she reached for a dress with daisy pockets.

7

Flora arrived at the Rosetown Free Library at nine Monday morning to help Mr. Anderson set up the craft table before the three-year-olds began arriving. She wanted to make a good impression, so she wore her navy-blue jumper and white blouse, which her mother admired as "crisp and professional." Flora hoped so. It was one thing to help in the back room of a paper shop sorting out birthday cards, and quite another to be responsible for a little child's entire craft experience. She wanted to look like someone a toddler could count on.

Mr. Anderson was pleased to see her.

"Good morning, Flora!" He beamed at her. "Are you ready to get started? We need lettuces and carrots and paper pails to put them in. Here, let me show you."

And just like that, Flora stepped from the old to the new. Here she was, by herself, being Flora in a different way. She could hardly believe it. This thing she was doing alone.

She stood with a pair of scissors before the boxes of green and orange construction paper and felt a sudden swell of happiness. She could hardly wait for the toddlers to arrive.

When they did arrive, the toddlers all seemed so small to Flora. She was not often around three-year-olds, and here they were, so little and shy. She was charmed.

And she put away all of her own natural shyness. It just wouldn't do if she were a person who held back at Toddler Story Time. She understood that these children needed reassurance and friendliness.

So she smiled at each of them, and at their parents, and she asked the names of the dolls and bears and bunnies who had come along. She gently led the way to the Story Time Corner and made sure each toddler was nicely settled and ready for a parent to move away and head toward the Adult Reading Room, provided there were no tears.

And not a single tear fell. Mr. Anderson was already sitting in his Story Time chair, and he was holding a cardboard box on his lap. All of the children who had attended Story Time before were excited to see this box because they knew who was in it: a corgi dog named Toasty.

Toasty was actually a puppet—though much more than that to these children—and when the big funny ears began to come up from inside the box, the Children's Room was suddenly bright with happiness. Story Time had begun.

Mr. Anderson first entertained the children with Toasty. Then, when the corgi went back into his box to take a nap, Mr. Anderson began reading them a picture book, holding it open so everyone could see the pictures. During this time Flora stood quietly beside the craft table, counting the number of toddler heads and comparing it to the number of paper pails. There were enough. As for the lettuces and carrots, she was sure there were enough of those to feed everyone in Rosetown.

When Mr. Anderson finished the story of Peter Rabbit, the toddlers all moved to the table, leaving their dolls and bears and bunnies behind to nap with Toasty. They were ready for paper and glue.

Flora did her best. Three-year-olds move quite quickly when presented with a table full of lettuces and carrots and glue sticks. Flora helped them fill up their paper pails with garden vegetables, guiding their small hands with her own, reapplying glue as needed, and picking up whatever floated to the floor. Only once did she have to remind them that the vegetables were not real, so children could not eat them, but dolls and bunnies and bears could.

The children went home with pails and books, and Flora felt a great sense of accomplishment. As she helped Mr. Anderson tidy up, he thanked her for her "good help and good cheer." She left the library in a bit of a daze.

Later that day Flora and Nessy compared notes about their Mondays.

"They gave me a T-shirt at music camp," Nessy told Flora on the phone.

"They did?" asked Flora.

"Yes," said Nessy. "It's blue and there's a treble clef on the front and my name on the back. I'm supposed to wear it every day."

"That's so nice!" said Flora.

"I guess they thought I was taller, because it comes down to my knees," said Nessy. "But that's okay."

Sweet Nessy. "But that's okay" was something she said so often that it could almost have been her motto.

"I didn't get a T-shirt," said Flora, "but one of the toddlers gave me his paper garden pail after craft time."

"He did?" asked Nessy. "That means you're his favorite."

"They were all really good," said Flora. "They

like glue sticks a lot. And I had to explain that they aren't supposed to eat the lettuces and carrots."

"That's what I would have done when I was three," said Nessy. "I ate everything."

"Did you love music camp, Nessy?" asked Flora.

"I think I'll love it tomorrow," Nessy answered. "I was too nervous today. But everyone was so nice. We're going to be a little orchestra! And give a concert for people on Friday."

"I'll come!" said Flora.

"There are a lot of big instruments. Like a bassoon," said Nessy. "I didn't know what a bassoon was until today."

"I don't know what a bassoon is," said Flora.

"Oh, just come to the concert," said Nessy, "and I'll show you."

Flora smiled. Nessy was sounding very sure about music camp.

"But I missed Sunny," said Nessy. "Did you miss Serenity?"

"Yes," Flora said. "She was sleeping in the bookcase when I got home. On top of the Monopoly game."

"I can't play Monopoly very well," said Nessy. "But I like the little dog."

"Me too," said Flora.

"Do you remember the story of Peter Rabbit?" Flora asked Nessy.

"Sure," said Nessy. "He squeezed under the gate."

"He did," said Flora. "Mr. Anderson read it to the toddlers today, and they listened to every word. Two little girls held hands while they listened."

"That was us," said Nessy with a giggle.

After she finished talking with Nessy, Flora went out to the porch to sit. Serenity followed and jumped up into her lap and began to purr. Serenity loved porch time.

Flora could hear her father and mother making dinner in the kitchen. She could smell potatoes frying on the stove. They would have fresh sliced tomatoes with them. They always did. And squash. Their garden was small, but Peter Rabbit would have loved it.

Then Flora thought about Montana. And wondered how big the gardens grew there.

8

Flora had never been inside Rosetown High School, and when the day of Nessy's concert arrived, Flora wondered what she should wear. She didn't want to look too young. High school students intrigued her, they were so confident and stylish, and she didn't want to seem an awkward child among them. When Flora told her mother she was nervous about being in the midst of so many teenagers, her mother replied, "Oh, I think the audience will be mostly parents, dear. The high school kids will probably be at the movies." This information reassured Flora somewhat and also further added to her curiosity about the life of a teenager: she wondered what movie they would go see.

But today was about Nessy, who had spent the week with music students of all ages and was about to make the leap from piano recital to concert. Sunny and Happy Girl would have to wait at home: Nessy was going onstage!

When Flora and her parents arrived at the high school, they walked through the front door of the building and down the hallway leading to the auditorium, where the concert would take place. Flora was excited to see the interior of Rosetown High for the first time. It seemed to her a place of very serious learning. And it was so big compared to the elementary school. She loved the flights of stairs, the rows of lockers, the glass display cases filled with trophies. She wanted to go into the classrooms and see the kinds of books teenagers read.

"I think I'll like high school," she told her parents.

"Most people do," her father said. "It's a very alive time."

A very alive time. Flora wondered what that would mean for her, for Nessy, for Yury. Flora loved the past: old houses, old towns, old ways of life. But walking through this building, she felt a new interest in the future.

"I'll probably join a lot of clubs," she said.

They arrived at the entrance to the auditorium, where two students handed them programs. Then they found some seats near the stage. Many people were saying hello to one another, mothers and fathers sharing their excitement. Flora's mother was right: there were many parents, and some young children, and the teenagers were at the movies. Flora spotted Nessy's parents near the back corner, with Nessy's older brother, Michael. Flora rarely saw him when she visited Nessy's house because he was always busy with his activities. Michael would go away to college soon. But today he was here for his sister, not at the movies.

The seats were filled, and the program began.

First the conductor stepped out from behind the curtains, baton in hand, and told the audience how wonderful it had been to work with "these very special musicians." She told them how important music education was and that all children everywhere should have the opportunity to play an instrument if they wished to learn. She said that music brings happiness.

Then the heavy velvet curtains behind her opened, and there were all the young musicians.

Nessy! Flora could hardly believe it, but there was her friend.

Nessy was seated at one of six pianos, holding herself very straight and looking only at the conductor. Like the other musicians, she was wearing black and white. Being Nessy, she had added a large white bow to her hair.

Flora grabbed her mother's hand. This was important. This would be a memory.

The conductor lifted her baton, and the music began, filling the auditorium with the beautiful opening sound of violins.

When the concert was over, there were many "Bravos," and Nessy stood up and took a bow with the rest of the orchestra members. Then the curtains closed and the young musicians scattered to find their families and friends.

Nessy found Flora before she found her brother and parents. Flora handed Nessy the small bunch of daisies she had brought.

"Thank you," said Nessy. "Were we groovy?" She giggled.

"You were so good!" Flora said. Her mother gave Nessy a hug, and Flora's father applauded and said another "Bravo" for good measure.

"I'd better go find my family," said Nessy. "We're going to get milkshakes!"

She hugged Flora, then hurried away into the crowd of excited musicians and parents. As Flora watched her go, she remembered that Nessy had taken piano lessons last year because Flora had asked that they do it together. And here Nessy was, in her black and white, her name in a concert program—*Vanessa* instead of *Nessy*—listed as one of the *very special musicians* in Rosetown.

Flora was proud of her friend.

"Did that word 'milkshake' sound good to you?" she asked her parents with a smile.

9

Saturday was graduation day for the Beginner class at the Good Manners for Good Dogs dog school, and the families of the graduates were appropriately excited. Completing a challenging course of learning is difficult enough for anyone, but when the student of that course is someone who would like nothing more than to roll around in dirt in the backyard and to chew on the leg of the coffee table in the living room, achieving a certificate of learning is a feat close to landing on the moon.

But somehow twenty good dogs did just that. They faithfully attended school every Saturday morning for ten weeks, leashing up to their devoted owners and learning to heel, to stay, to sit, to wait, and to amaze the world with their good manners. They earned a lot of mini-biscuits. And Friday was one of those dogs.

Friday had been born in a litter of puppies birthed at the home of a patient of Yury's father. Yury's family had not been thinking about getting a dog. They were fairly new in town and were still thinking mostly of getting completely unpacked. It had been a long, strange journey from their country of the Ukraine to this small town in Indiana. Yury's parents had not meant to leave the Ukraine permanently, only long enough for Yury's father to get additional medical training at a university in Chicago.

But, as sometimes happens to a family, events in the larger world decided the course their family would take. Unrest overwhelmed the Ukraine, and after four years away, it was too dangerous to return home. So Yury's parents, with the help of many kindnesses from others, found a way to stay in America, keeping their son safe. They eventually moved to Rosetown, Indiana.

Then Yury had met Flora on the first day of school, and the two friends met a stray cat who had no name but would soon have not only a name but also a warm bed by a sunny window and an owner devoted to her: Flora.

Yury's parents heard all about the rescue of the white cat with a yellow tip on her tail. Yury seemed to talk of nothing else for days. The family had once had a cat of its own—Juliette—when Yury was younger. But Juliette died of old age when she was sixteen. And the family had been so busy since then that another pet seemed unlikely anytime soon.

But Yury talked so much about the stray cat.

And not long after, one of the patients of Yury's father mentioned—between the taking of temperature and blood pressure—that his beloved collie was about to have her first litter of pups. The man was visibly joyful—which fortunately did not raise his blood pressure—and with pride described building a whelping box for his collie to give birth in.

So there were, in Yury's household, suddenly many thoughts about dogs and cats.

There were so many of those thoughts that Yury's father finally asked his patient if he might have one of those puppies for his boy, Yury, who was new in Rosetown and had only one friend so far—a nice girl named Flora—and who might like one more.

That is how Friday came to Yury. And part of Yury's responsibility to this new puppy, Yury's parents told him, would be Saturday mornings at the Good Manners for Good Dogs dog school.

Friday was first enrolled in puppy class, and for many Saturdays he tumbled around with the other puppies and learned about leashes, and the eyes and voice of his owner, and about being comfortable in a puppy carrier when it was time to go into the car or take a nap.

Flora had met up with Yury and Friday every

Saturday at puppy class. She loved watching all of the puppies.

And now, after a summer of Beginner class, which Flora had also faithfully visited, Friday would receive his first obedience-trained-dog certificate.

The ceremony was to take place in the same large space where the dogs had so carefully learned to be good. Folding chairs were arranged for friends and family, just as for any graduation.

As always, on Saturday morning Yury and Friday met Flora in front of Rosetown Hardware, to walk around to the dog school in back. Yury was wearing a carefully ironed button-down shirt and creased slacks, clothes denoting the importance of the occasion. Friday was groomed and brushed, not a tangle to be seen in his collie coat. And Flora wore a summer dress and new yellow sandals.

"Ready?" asked Yury.

"Ready," said Flora, giving Friday an encouraging pat on the head.

Inside she took a seat on a folding chair next to

Yury's parents, who were already there. She shyly said hello. As did they.

Then they watched together as Yury and Friday and all of the other good owners and good dogs showed everyone what they had learned about watching, listening, obeying—and being best friends.

Yury was so composed throughout. Flora watched him, and she could see the future person he would be: capable and calm. She knew he would help others, as he so wanted to do. As long as it didn't bore him.

When the demonstrations were finished, the class instructors gave each owner a certificate and each dog a mini-biscuit. There was much applause and sometimes a "Hurray!"

After the graduation was over, Flora and Yury said good-bye to his parents and walked to the bakery with Friday as usual. Yury rolled up the sleeves of his formal shirt, ready to be comfortable again.

Flora admired Friday's certificate.

"It looks a lot like the one on the wall in your father's office," she said.

"Except Friday worked harder for his," Yury answered with a grin.

They ate their muffins quietly for a bit, each gathering back some energy after the exciting morning.

Then Yury said, "I changed my mind about the Boy Scouts."

"You did?" asked Flora.

"It seems that I would join the Cub Scouts first," Yury continued, "and attend a lot of meetings and tie knots."

"Knots," repeated Flora.

"It's one thing at a time in Scouts," said Yury. "Then after I finish fifth grade, I can join the Boy Scouts."

He paused.

"You know how impatient I am," Yury said.

Flora nodded.

"I think I can learn a lot from Survivor Bob on my own," said Yury, "and not have to wait around."

Yury had all the Survivor Bob books.

"You'd make friends with other Cub Scouts," said Flora. "You might like that."

"Probably none of them would know as much about edible plants as you do," Yury answered, handing Friday half of his second muffin.

"Probably," agreed Flora.

"Besides, I have friends in the Archery Club," said Yury.

"Right," Flora agreed.

"My father said he can teach me how to bandage, and other first aid skills," Yury continued. "He said I don't have to wear a uniform but I do have to wash the dishes twice a week."

"That sounds fair," Flora said. "And if you pick up a knife the wrong way, you'll know how to bandage yourself."

"I thought of that," said Yury.

They were quiet again. Friday had fallen asleep on Yury's shoes.

"If Wings and a Chair closes," Yury finally said, "we'll have to find something else to read besides vintage books. I suppose we could try Mars Comics."

Flora didn't want to think about Wings and a Chair closing, and she especially didn't want to think about Mars Comics and its grumpy owner. He seemed to be annoyed by kids, who were the number one customers in his shop. Besides, Yury was the person who loved comics. Not her.

"I don't think so," she said.

They were quiet again.

"Well, do you have any ideas?" he asked.

Flora shook her head. "No ideas. But did you know that the Sweet Shoppe has a new ice cream?" she asked. "It's in the colors of the high school. Tiger Swirl."

"Blue-and-gold ice cream definitely sounds interesting," said Yury.

Whatever the future might hold, they both felt pretty sure Tiger Swirl would be a part of it.

10

Back in December, when Miss Meriwether had returned from her Christmas trip to Paris, she had brought Flora a necklace that held a tiny elephant charm. It wasn't a brand-new necklace. It was from a Paris flea market, which made it all the more special. Miss Meriwether knew that Flora would most love something old.

Flora regarded this necklace as something so meaningful that she had carefully put it away and planned to wear it only on special occasions.

So why she decided to start wearing it every day

during these ordinary last days of summer, Flora wasn't sure. One morning she opened a dresser drawer, removed the box, and put the necklace around her neck. And now she did this every morning.

There is a meaning to some things that a person cannot always define. When an object has some link to the heart, it is often because it came from someone dear or was loved by someone dear who has passed away. Or sometimes the object is a treasured reminder of an experience: a winning game, the first sight of the ocean, a project carried through with intense devotion.

Flora began wearing the elephant necklace, though she did not know exactly why.

Flora and Yury were now making August morning visits to the bookshop because Yury's afternoons were taken. He was helping his father repaint the office, and painting began once the last appointment of the day was finished. In a doctor's office, this could be unpredictable.

Miss Meriwether was always happy to see them,

and they were happy to step inside. The old wood floors shone beautifully in the morning sunlight. The store was quiet, this early. And everywhere were books.

Both Flora and Yury loved talking to Miss Meriwether. She was keenly interested in their lives: What were their favorite songs? What were they watching on television? Reading?

And sometimes Miss Meriwether surprised Flora with her quiet observations. She once said to Flora, "You remind me of the young French girls who sew beautiful lace collars and think about life." This pleased Flora, who thought herself mostly ordinary and plain. Being compared to anything French was nice.

And on another day, when Flora was in the shop while her mother was there working, Miss Meriwether made another unexpected observation: "Yury has a power no one can see."

Flora was startled when she heard this. Because Miss Meriwether was right. Flora had always known this about Yury. She just had not had the words for it. Miss Meriwether seemed able to see more than just the surface of a person.

On each visit to the shop this summer, Flora and Yury had watched for some sign, some clue from Miss Meriwether about the decision she would make about leaving or staying. But Miss Meriwether gave up no information, directly or indirectly.

"She would make a good detective," Yury remarked when they had left the shop one morning. "She's as hard to read as Columbo."

Yury never missed an episode of *Columbo* on television.

After Flora had promised Nessy she would ask Miss Meriwether about Indianapolis, she had stopped by the shop the next day to talk about the conservatory and a possible visit. Flora was reluctant to ask people for favors, but here she was, ready to do just that, the result of persuading Nessy to attend music camp.

Miss Meriwether was just finishing up a sale with a customer at the counter.

"I love a good mystery too," she was saying to the

gentleman. "Have you read Agatha Christie?"

The gentleman said he had not.

"I'll put something of hers aside for your next visit," said Miss Meriwether. "She spins quite a story."

Spins quite a story. Flora knew writers who did that. She had found them in Wings and a Chair. Some were like old friends.

When the customer had gone, Miss Meriwether said a cheerful hello to Flora, giving her a quick hug.

"How are you today, dear Flora? And your sweet kitty?" asked Miss Meriwether.

Flora smiled. "We're very well," she answered. "Serenity has discovered she can jump to the top of our Hoosier cabinet."

"Cats do love high places," said Miss Meriwether. "One of my friends, years ago in New York, built cat shelves all along the top of her walls. Then she and the cats moved to the country, where there were trees. She hardly saw them after that except at dinnertime. They were always in a tree. And, unlike most cats, could get themselves down again."

"Serenity hasn't tried a tree," said Flora.

"Probably for the best," answered Miss Meriwether with a smile. "We wouldn't want to call out a fire truck for Miss Kitty."

Flora smiled. Miss Meriwether was so easy to talk to. And because she was, Flora found the courage to ask her question.

"I came to see you today," Flora began, "because Nessy and I were wondering . . ."

No, that's not what I mean to say, she thought. She started over.

"Nessy is going to music camp at the high school this week," she said.

"Wonderful!" said Miss Meriwether. "So brave for a shy girl like Nessy. But the piano gives her courage, don't you think?"

"It does!" answered Flora.

She continued:

"And I was wondering if after Nessy's camp is finished and if you have time and if it sounds like fun . . ."

Flora took a breath.

". . . if you would like to go to the conservatory in Indianapolis with us. In your car. But we could bring the car snacks," she finished. Then she added, "Nessy likes those orange circus peanuts."

Miss Meriwether gave her a big smile.

"I love those too!" she said. "Of course! Let's have an adventure in Indianapolis! If all the parents say yes. I'll promise them that you and Nessy will learn all about tropical horticulture."

"Nessy especially loves horticulture," said Flora. "Horticulture" was a word she had never used until now, and she liked it. She assumed it meant "plants."

"Nessy will be so excited."

"I'm excited already!" said Miss Meriwether.

And easy as that, the trip had been set.

Flora loved Miss Meriwether. And lately Miss Meriwether seemed to be shining in a special way. Flora searched her mind for the word.

Luminous. Lately Miss Meriwether was luminous.

11

On their way to the conservatory in Indianapolis, Flora and Nessy told Miss Meriwether all about their new adventures involving toddlers and bassoons.

"Nessy did so well in the concert," Flora said. "She even had a solo."

"For ten seconds," Nessy said with a giggle.

"That's only because they had to let the other pianos have a solo too," said Flora. "There were a lot of pianos."

"Plus other instruments," added Nessy.

"It was really good," said Flora.

They were traveling in Miss Meriwether's Honda Civic. In 1973 the small cars from Japan were becoming popular, and it was exciting for both girls to be traveling in one. Flora's parents were still driving the same large car Flora's father had had in college, which he sometimes called the Boat. Flora could not imagine Miss Meriwether in a Boat.

Before long they saw the tall buildings of Indianapolis up ahead. The nice thing about flat land is being able to always see what is up ahead. Miss Meriwether knew just where she was going. They drove through a beautiful park graced by fountains and flower gardens and tidy sidewalks on which people strolled, some pushing baby carriages and some holding hands or just chatting.

Then just beyond this beautiful park and around a slow curve, before Flora and Nessy were even prepared to see it, there stood the conservatory.

Flora and Nessy couldn't help themselves: they squealed.

Miss Meriwether laughed and said, "I thought

I was dreaming when I first saw it too. I was just about your age."

The conservatory was an enormous building, and its roof and its walls were all made of glass. Inside it the girls could see, even from the car, giant palm trees growing all the way to the top. A tropical landscape under glass.

When finally they stepped into this magical glass house, for a moment the girls were silent.

Then Flora said, "This is the nicest air I have ever tasted."

Everywhere, all around them, the conservatory was thick with exotic plants and trees they had never seen before, never imagined. Some leaves of the plants were so large that they seemed prehistoric, as if a dinosaur might suddenly step out from behind them.

"Look, Nessy," said Flora, pointing to a palm with a thick batch of long, hair-like strands sprouting from it.

"*Old Man Palm*," Nessy read aloud from the information marker. "I think he could use a haircut."

Flora laughed.

They followed the meandering brick pathways throughout the conservatory, often stopping simply to gaze up at the roof of glass, so high, with so much blue sky.

Miss Meriwether pointed toward a small tropical tree with blue star-shaped flowers.

"Look, Flora," she said. "It's a Tree of Life."

Flora read the marker. "It says that the resin is used for healing," Flora said. "I'll tell Yury."

The three wandered slowly and dreamily through the lush, moist forest of stunning palms and ferns and giant cacti. They touched their fingers to the cool, dark water of small pools filled with giant lily pads. Even with visitors, the conservatory was quiet, with voices hushed, everyone respectful of this world.

Eventually it was time for lunch. Miss Meriwether led the girls to the café and to one of the bistro tables located on a stone patio beside a small waterfall. Since the girls were uncertain about what to order, Miss Meriwether asked the waiter for a large plate of tea sandwiches they could all share and a pitcher of iced hibiscus flower tea.

"Miss Meriwether, I thought of you while I was looking at the Ponytail Palm," Nessy said with a playful smile.

Miss Meriwether laughed.

Sandwiches and tea arrived, beautifully presented with palm leaf plates and water lily tumblers. Everyone was quite hungry, and the food was very welcome.

"I want to be a gardener more than ever now," said Nessy. "Is it okay to put sugar in the tea?"

"All the sugar you like," Miss Meriwether said, smiling. "And what will you grow in your garden?"

"Really tall sunflowers," answered Nessy.

"Sunflowers are rather like people, I've always thought," said Miss Meriwether.

"They are!" said Nessy. "I would give each one a name."

"You can't name anyone Sunny," Flora said. "Somebody already has that name!"

Nessy giggled.

"I'm learning all the flowers from a book I have," said Nessy. "Hydrangea, foxglove, gladiolus . . . There are a lot of flowers."

"Fabulous," said Miss Meriwether. "I always liked four-o'clocks."

"Me too!" said Nessy. "They're in my book too!"

"You could put birdhouses in your garden," said Flora. "The birds could eat the sunflower seeds and be Sunny's neighbors."

"Yes!" said Nessy.

"Someday I hope you can visit a Japanese garden," said Miss Meriwether. "They are meant to be places for reflection, so they are very simple, with rocks, water, lanterns.

"And no four-o'clocks," she added with a smile.

"I love these tea sandwiches," said Flora. "And the pretty plates."

"Small beautiful things," said Miss Meriwether. "They make life nicer, I think."

"I think so too," said Nessy. "When I have my little cottage and flower garden, I'm going to invite you and Flora for tea and tea sandwiches."

"Lovely!" said Miss Meriwether.

"I'm sure I can do it," Nessy continued. "Just boil the water and cut off the crusts."

They all laughed then, Miss Meriwether most of all.

On the way back home to Rosetown, everyone was a little tired and a little quiet, which gave Flora time for her thoughts. It occurred to her that sometimes when one knows a person in only a certain setting—a bookshop, for instance—one can't imagine how to spend time with that person in any other way. Flora remembered going with her mother for dinner at Miss Meriwether's apartment in the Victorian house last winter. It had been fun and interesting—Flora learned about the prayer flags in the Himalayas—but she had depended on her mother to do the real visiting, to carry on the real conversation. Even though they hadn't been in the bookshop, still they'd worn their certain roles: Owner, Part-Time Employee, Part-Time Employee's Daughter Who Visits the Bookshop Quite a Lot.

But today, at the conservatory, Miss Meriwether

had seemed more like a friend of the family, even part of the family. Could she become an auntie? Flora wondered about this. Was it possible for someone to be a certain sort of person for a while— bookshop owner—and then somewhere in the middle of things change into another sort of person: an auntie from Montana?

For Flora, who relied more than most on constancy, this thought was not too troubling when the person in a new role might be Miss Meriwether. If Flora's life was like a house, Miss Meriwether was not really part of the foundation, holding the house steady and strong. She was more like a flower in the garden. If Miss Meriwether went away to Montana, and came back for visits, the house would still be all right.

But there were some people in Flora's life who were the foundation of the house: her mother and father and Nessy. All were constant and depended upon. Flora needed them.

And Yury . . .

Flora finally realized that the true reason why

she needed Miss Meriwether to stay was because her bookshop was the foundation upon which Flora and Yury had built their friendship. The shelves of books, the Young People's Nook, and Miss Meriwether had all held this friendship steady and strong.

And Flora was afraid that if Miss Meriwether disappeared, and the bookshop with her, Yury would disappear as well.

This was why Flora had been wearing the elephant charm around her neck. To keep Miss Meriwether—and him—from leaving.

12

During the final week of August, everyone in Rosetown was reminded that the new school year was about to begin, because of all the noise coming from the football field at the high school. In the mornings the marching band had started practicing, and the loud rap-rapping of the snare drums could be heard by all who passed by. And in the afternoons when the football team arrived to practice, the frantic tweets of the coach's whistle confirmed that the sleepy days of summer vacation would soon be over.

Yury and Flora met at the central park one morning during that week to give Friday a chance to do some practicing of his own: obedience skills in a public place. The park presented Friday with many canine temptations, most of them with four feet and bushy tails.

"What if he runs away?" Flora asked Yury as they walked to a grassy open area in the middle of the park.

"I'll run faster," said Yury. "But he won't. He's a good listener."

Yury came to a sudden stop. Friday stopped too. So did Flora. For a moment she thought, *This must be what it feels like to be a dog in training.*

Yury looked down at Friday.

"Watch," he said.

Friday looked up at him.

"Wait," said Yury. Then he carefully released the leash from Friday's collar.

"Stay," Yury said. He then walked several paces away from Friday. Flora was looking out for squirrels.

"Friday, *come!*" Yury called.

Friday ran straight to Yury, circled around him, then stood at his left side in heel position.

Yury gave Friday a mini-biscuit.

"Good dog!" Yury and Flora said together. Flora clapped her hands. She had not dared move until now.

"Eventually I'll be able to walk all the way over there by the fountain while Friday stays here," Yury told Flora as he leashed Friday up again.

"He didn't take his eyes off you," said Flora.

They walked together to the large fountain. A special spigot just for dogs was next to it, and Yury filled the concrete basin beneath it with water. After Friday finished drinking, Yury and Flora settled on the edge of the fountain while Friday lay down at their feet.

"The Intermediate class is next," Yury said. "In November."

"Right," said Flora.

"But the hardest class will be Advanced Obedience," said Yury.

"Yes," said Flora. "Hand signals."

"Hand signals are important for Search and Rescue," said Yury. "I wouldn't want to stir up any grizzlies by yelling 'Sit!'"

Flora smiled.

"Did you buy school clothes yet?" she asked.

"No," answered Yury, "but I got some mechanical pencils. They're great."

"You just like saying 'mechanical,'" said Flora.

"It does sound impressive," Yury said.

They were quiet. Friday sat up to give his full attention to a squirrel running down a nearby tree.

"Only two more weeks until Miss Meriwether leaves," Flora said finally.

Yury looked at her. "That soon? I can hardly believe it," he answered.

"My mother had her to our house on Sunday for cinnamon rolls," Flora said. "Miss Meriwether told us that she might get married," Flora said.

"What?" said Yury with a look of surprise.

"Her friend in Montana," said Flora, "was a boy she knew right here, in Rosetown, when they were growing up."

"Really?" asked Yury.

"His name is Robert," said Flora. "She liked him a lot. But when they graduated, he joined the Navy, and she went to India. She didn't know where he was for years. Then one day after last Christmas, his father walked into the bookshop."

"Wow," said Yury. "And . . . ?"

"And he told her that Robert was living in Montana. So she wrote to him. And he wrote back. They wrote a lot. She said they wrote fifteen years of letters in three months."

"Amazing," said Yury.

"She needs to go," said Flora.

Yury nodded.

"She said that someone might buy the bookshop," Flora added. "Rosetown really needs a bookshop."

Yury nodded again. Then he looked at Flora.

"I was thinking," he said, "that maybe we could try something totally new. While we're waiting to see what happens to the shop."

"Really?" asked Flora. "What?"

"Horseback riding," said Yury.

Flora looked at him, her eyes wide with surprise.

"There's a stable outside of town," Yury said. "I asked my mother, she said she can drop us off and pick us up."

"Horses?" asked Flora. Horses were so beautiful.

"We should learn how to ride," said Yury.

He waited for Flora to say something.

"Do you remember that book *The Mystery Horse*?" asked Flora finally.

"I do, but I didn't read it," Yury said. "You're the one who loves the horse stories. You're the one who loves horses."

You're the one who loves horses. Flora silently repeated the words.

Then she realized that Yury wanted to take riding lessons for her. He wanted this for her.

"Did you know that people used to ride horses to the bank in Rosetown?" she asked him. She would have to think all of her many thoughts later.

"You have told me that a million times," said Yury with a smile.

Flora smiled too. They had spent a lot of time

together if a story had been shared a million times. A lot of time. Enough for a foundation.

Flora bent over and gave Friday a big hug.

Maybe someday she would take Yury to see the Tree of Life.

But for now it was almost time to start fifth grade.

What a beautiful day this was. In Rosetown, Indiana.

Cynthia Rylant grew up in West Virginia and then spent many years living in the Midwest. Today she lives with her cat, Benjamin, in an old, green house in Oregon.